T0198987

TUNA

Black Jackie

By Trudy L. Himes

This Book Belongs to:

_____

Book Designer: Jerome Cuyos

To order additional copies of this book, contact:
Xlibris
844-714-8691
www.Xlibris.com
Orders@Xlibris.com

ISBN: Softcover   978-1-5992-6614-5
        Hardcover   978-1-5992-6621-3

Library of Congress Control Number: 2005907935

Print information available on the last page

Rev. date: 01/12/2023

Black Jackie

Written & illustrated

by

Trudy L. Himes

Black Jackie

Jackie is my cat of black
He sometimes wears a hat.
He sleeps away each sunny day.
I think he's getting fat!

Of all the foods that Jackie loves,
Tuna tops his list.
He leaves the others to get dry
and ignores my shaking fist!

Jackie loves to go outside
and munch upon the grass.
He climbs up in the tallest trees
and mocks my fears with sass!

Jackie doesn't sleep at night.
He'd rather roam about.
Until the sun is hanging high
and mice are hard to route.

But if he sleeps upon my feet,
I dare not move at all.
For if he wakes in early morn
He'll scratch upon my wall!

To a soul as free as his.
A car ride brings distaste.
Inside he circles endlessly
and exits it in haste.

Jackie is my friend so true.
He sets my heart aglow.
He never-ever deviates,
Except the seeds of hunt to sow!

When I scratch him on the head
and again upon his rump,
I see a smile upon his face
That takes away my frumps!

I love to kiss my Jackie-cat
and I know he'd kiss me too.
But Alas! You see, my Jackie-cat
No lips has he. - It's True!

t. l. himes

Jackie is my cat of
black.

He sometimes wears
a HAT!

He sleeps away each
sunny day.

I think he's getting
fat!

Of all the foods that
Jackie **loves**...

Tuna tops his list.

He leaves the "others" to get dry

And ignores my **Shaking** fist!

Jackie **loves** to go outside

And munch upon the grass.

TUNA

He climbs up in the **tallest** trees

And mocks my fears with sass!

Jackie doesn't sleep at night.

He'd rather roam **about**.

Until the **SUN** is hanging high

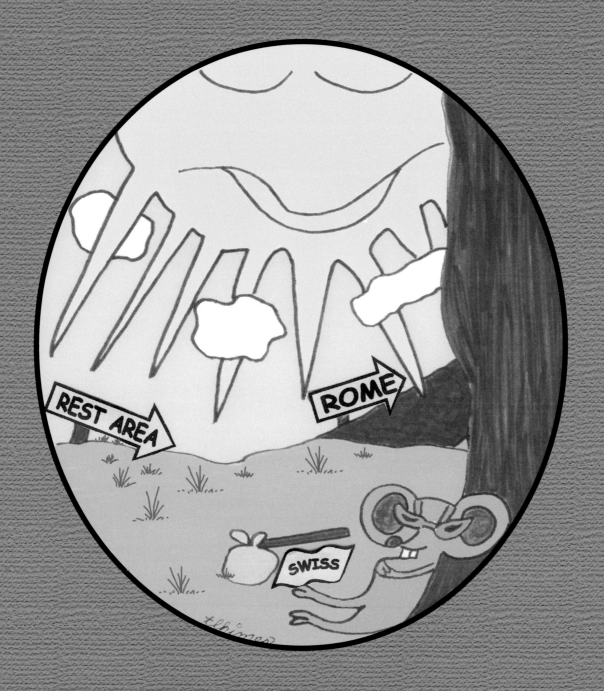

And mice are hard to route!

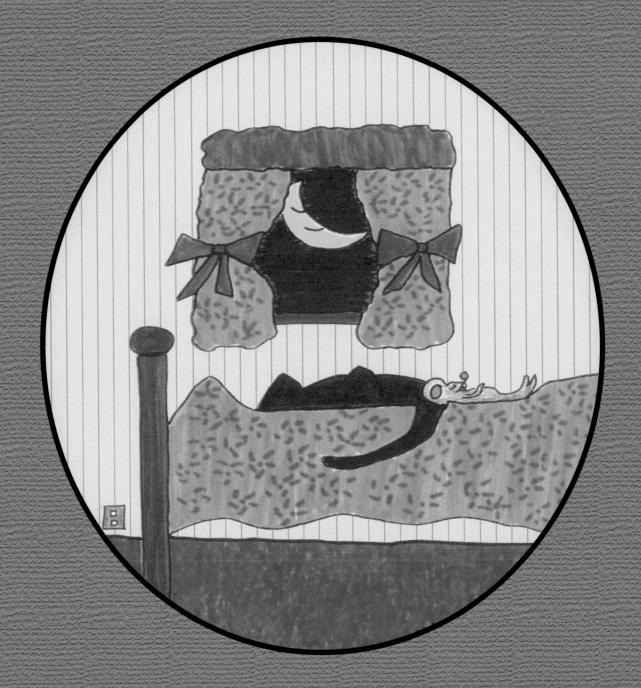

But If he sleeps upon my **feet,**

I dare not move **AT ALL!**

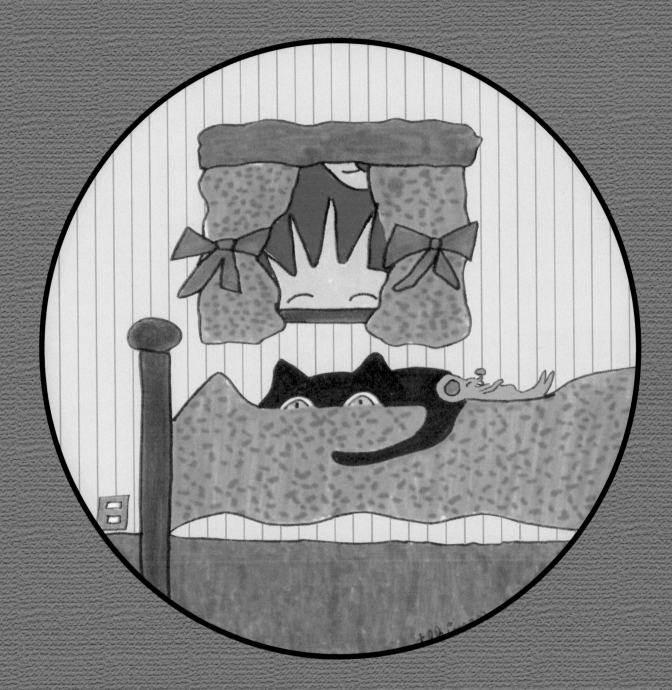

For if he wakes in **early morn**

He'll scratch upon **my** wall!

To a **soul** as free as his,

A car ride brings distaste.

Inside he **circles** endlessly

And exits it in **haste!**

Jackie is my friend so true.

He sets my **heart** aglow.

He **never-ever** deviates,

Except the seeds of hunt to sow!

When I scratch him on the head

And again upon his rump,

TUNA

I see a smile upon his face

That takes away my **frumps**!

I love to kiss my Jackie-Cat

And I know he'd **kiss** me too!

TUNA

But alas! You see, my Jackie - Cat

no lips has he !

It's True!

THE END

Printed in the United States
by Baker & Taylor Publisher Services